5 reasons you'll love this book

Join Maya as she flies through the air to save the day

Meet the beautiful birds of the kingdom and their fairy friends

The natural world is full of wonder—turn to the back for fascinating facts!

Get ready to meet the most amazing singers in the world!

Colouring in has never been so magical!

To the keeper of this book—it's time
for you to visit the magical kingdom
waiting within. Believe in yourself—that
will give you wings to fly!

For my lovely, musical and music-loving husband and children, music teachers everywhere, and all those who work to help songbirds. Thank you for the music!

OXFORD
UNIVERSITY PRESS

Great Clarendon Street, Oxford OX2 6DP
Oxford University Press is a department of the University of Oxford.
It furthers the University's objective of excellence in research, scholarship,
and education by publishing worldwide. Oxford is a registered trade mark of
Oxford University Press in the UK and in certain other countries

British Library Cataloguing in Publication Data

Data available

ISBN: 978-0-19-276627-4

1 3 5 7 9 10 8 6 4 2

Printed in India
Paper used in the production of this book is a natural,
recyclable product made from wood grown in sustainable forests.
The manufacturing process conforms to the environmental
regulations of the country of origin.

Javan Green Magpie
Contributor: Rebecca Cave / Alamy Stock Photo

Sumatran laughingthrush / black-and-white laughingthrush (Garrulax bicolor)
endemic to the Indonesian island of Sumatra
Contributor: Arterra Picture Library / Alamy Stock Photo

Other birds images from Shutterstock

Magical Kingdom
of Birds
The Silent Songbirds

ANNE BOOTH
Illustrated by Rosie Butcher

OXFORD
UNIVERSITY PRESS

Chapter One

Maya and her best friend Saffron were waiting to be picked up after school. They had been at choir practice together.

'It's so amazing that they want us both to sing solos,' said Saffron. 'But you looked a bit unhappy today when they told us. Are you feeling all right?'

'I don't know,' said Maya. 'At first I

was really excited to get a solo like you, and Penny and Dad will be happy, but I just don't think I can do it. I'm not very confident about reading music. I know you have been helping me to learn what we have to sing in the choir, but it is hard. You are so used to playing the flute and singing solos at your church, but I don't do anything like that.'

'You mustn't worry. You can pick most of it up by ear, and I can always help you read the music for your solo piece too. You've got a beautiful voice, Maya,' said Saffron. 'I will sing your part, and teach you how to read when the notes go up and down. The music notes are there to help remind you, not scare you.'

'Thank you. But I still don't feel very confident singing in front of people.'

'Maya! You swim, and ride horses, and go ice skating, and you don't let problems with your legs stop you. You're the bravest person I know!' said Saffron.

'That doesn't mean I don't get scared,' said Maya, as Saffron's mum's car turned up the school drive. 'I'm just normal. I'm not brave about everything. I don't have to be brave and stand in front of everyone when I swim or skate or ride horses.'

'The thing is, you really shouldn't worry,' said Saffron. 'You are so good!'

Maya felt her tummy give a twist. 'Sorry, Saffron. Could we not talk about it any more for a bit?' she said, passing her crutches in to Saffron and getting into the car to sit next to her.

'What are you not talking about?' said Theo, Saffron's brother, who was sitting in the front next to their mum.

'Don't be nosy, Theo,' laughed his mum.

'You're as bad as Patch!' said Maya,

without thinking.

'Who is Patch?' said Theo.

'Oh just a nosy magpie I read about,'
said Maya quickly.

'That's funny. Theo and I saw a
magpie in your garden today,' said their
mum. 'He was hopping up and down
your garden path earlier almost as if he
was waiting for you to come home. He
obviously didn't know you were staying
late for choir!'

Hearing about the magpie waiting in
her garden made Maya's tummy feel
completely different. Bubbles of

excitement replaced the sinking feeling she had when she thought about singing. She couldn't wait to be dropped off to see if the magpie was still there, and as she waved her friends goodbye she looked around the front garden, but no cheeky black and white bird could be seen.

'Hello, Maya love,' said Penny, giving her a hug as she got in. 'How was choir?'

Maya made a bit of a face. 'I don't think I'm as good as the other soloists,' she said.

'I'm certain you are,' said Penny. 'But anyway, it's a concert, not a competition. It's not like one of your swimming competitions.'

'I still don't want people to laugh at me,' said Maya, a bit crossly.

'Why would anyone laugh at you?' said Penny. 'They wouldn't have given you a solo if you weren't good. Anyway, your dad will be home soon and dinner will be ready in half an hour. Do you want anything to drink before?'

'No, thanks. I think I'll just go and sort things out in my room for a bit,' said Maya, and she smiled at Penny.

'Fine. I'll give you a call when I need the table laying,' said Penny. 'And Maya, I got those latest swimming certificates you won framed—I hope you like where I put them.'

Maya went straight to her room. Penny had hung her swimming certificates on the wall next to the bird clock. Maya felt cheered up seeing them.

'At least I'm good at swimming,' she said. She went to her window to look in the back garden. Perhaps the magpie was there?

It wasn't.

She opened a beautiful book which was lying closed on her desk. It had a deep-blue cover decorated all over with lots of pictures of little gold birds, and the title, in gold too, said 'Magical Kingdom of Birds'. Inside were various gorgeous-coloured pictures of hummingbirds, and swans, and fairy-wrens, but after that the pages were blank.

'If only there was a picture I could colour in,' said Maya. 'Then I could get back into the Magical Kingdom and see Willow and Patch.'

This is what Maya could not explain to her best friends. Her mother had died when she was little, and had left her a magical colouring book. When a picture appeared for Maya to colour in, it meant that she was being summoned to the Magical Kingdom of Birds. There, Maya wasn't only a schoolgirl—she was known as the Keeper of the Book, and she had to help the fairy princess Willow and her friend Patch, the talking magpie, defeat Princess Willow's wicked Uncle Astor. He had taken Willow's throne and stolen and destroyed Willow's magical royal cloak, which had feathers from every bird in the kingdom, and Maya was helping Patch and Willow collect them all again. The problem was that she could only get into the kingdom when a new picture appeared, and she never knew when it would.

Maya went to sit on her bed with the

book. Suddenly she felt a tingling in her fingers as she held the book, and there, in front of her eyes, lines began to appear.

'A new picture!' she said, excitedly, and reached for the satchel hanging over the back of her chair, for the magical colouring pencils her mother had left her.

The picture revealed itself, but it was very odd. There was an open flute case with a flute inside it, lying on some blank pieces of paper. It seemed to be in the middle of a forest glade, and the surrounding trees were filled with lots of different kinds of birds. Tiny musical

notes filled the edges of the page. A silver
pencil rolled out of the case as if to say
'pick me'.

'I'd better colour in the flute, then,' said Maya, and started. As soon as she had finished, the flute in the case began to flash and sparkle so brightly that she had to blink. For a moment all she could see were silver music notes around her, and all she could hear was beautiful birdsong—warbles and flutes and whistles and tweets—as she was lifted up into the silver cloud. She felt herself getting smaller and smaller and then tumbling down towards and into the book, and found herself sitting on the ground in a hot tropical forest.

She was surrounded by incredible plants with beautiful flowers. They towered over her in the heat, and above her was a green canopy of leaves as far as she could see, filling the air with a soft green light. The warbles and squawks and laughing calls and tweets and flute-like birdsong around her was now so loud she did not hear Princess Willow at first, and jumped when she felt Willow's arms around her as she appeared from behind to give her a hug. Her black curls tickled Maya's cheek and Maya turned with a delighted smile.

'Oh Willow! It's so lovely to see you!' Maya shouted above the sounds. 'What's going on?'

'It's a songbird concert,' laughed Willow, coming to sit beside Maya. She was wearing a sparkling coronet which looked very beautiful against her dark hair.

'Of course!' said Maya. 'That's what all the musical notes were about!'

'What a cacophony!' said Patch.

'Pardon? And hello Patch!' said Maya, reaching up to give her friend a hug, his glossy sleek feathers shining, his black eyes bright and full of cleverness and fun.

'A cacophony. A din. A lot of noise,' said Patch, disapprovingly.

'Look over there at those bright green magpies practising,' said Willow, pointing towards two stunning little magpies with vivid green feathers. The black colouring on their faces made them look as if they were wearing bandit eye masks. They were very loud, squawking and squeaking and then making little noise patterns, whistling and making a grating noise at the end.

'I don't call that music,' said Patch,

derisively.

'They are certainly very confident,' said Maya, and smiled at him. Patch didn't seem to wish he could sing like his cheeky green cousins.

A small brown bird took off from the forest floor and flew up above them whistling sweetly and tunefully.

'That's a lark,' said Willow. 'Beautiful.'

'But what's a lark doing in a tropical forest?' asked Maya. 'I can see all sorts of birds who don't normally live here.'

'Yes, they've come from all over for the concert,' replied Willow. 'Uncle Astor invited them as a surprise for me.'

'What?' said Maya, worriedly. 'But I didn't think the birds would trust him to do that.'

'He wrote me such a lovely letter, Maya,' said Willow. 'He said he was playing his flute and the music reminded him of my mother, and he felt very sad. He says he is sorry for everything he has done and that he is turning over a new leaf. It's such good news, Maya! He says that he wants to be friends and that this singing gala will bring us together in a new way.'

Patch snorted. 'I'll believe that when I see it,' he said.

'I don't know if I would trust him so easily,' said Maya, worried. 'He destroyed your cloak and he has caused so much trouble.'

'People change,' said Princess Willow. 'I want to believe him. He was my mother Arly's brother, Maya. My mother was such a lovely singer and he used to accompany her on the flute. She used to sing me to sleep at night. I loved to listen to her.'

'My sister Lauren said my mum used

to sing me to sleep when I was a baby,'
said Maya. 'I don't remember her doing
it though.'

'I'll sing you a song,' said Willow.
'Listen.'

Here's a cloak of dreams, my sweetheart,
Coloured like the birds above,
Sparkling like the stars in night skies,
Feather-soft and full of love.

May your dreams be full of birdsong,
Brave adventures, friendship too,
Wrapped in feathers, sleep my darling,
Love will always be with you.

'That's so lovely,' said Maya. 'And knowing that there is a real cloak of feathers makes it even more special. I wish my dreams were full of birdsong, I love it.'

'It was my mother's special lullaby for me,' said Willow. 'And I love birdsong too, of course! No wonder we are special friends!' and they laughed and hugged each other. 'Look Maya, I brought your quiver and sticks with me, just in case you were here,' said Willow. 'I had a special feeling we would see you, didn't I, Patch? And I was right!'

'Well, Princess Willow, as you bring them with you everywhere we go,' said Patch, 'I think you had to be right some time!'

'You can't talk—you asked me to put on your harness today, and you only need it when Maya rides you! You must have believed me,' said Willow, laughing happily and flying off into the trees to chat to the birds, as Maya used her sticks to help her get up and then on to Patch's back.

'Princess Willow is right—I did think you would be here today,' said Patch over his shoulder as Maya put her sticks in her quiver and settled back. 'But because I think something is up. Like you, I don't trust her Uncle Astor as far as I can throw him. Something's wrong, I'm sure of it, but the Princess is so excited, and wants so badly to believe her uncle, that her guard is down. We need you, Maya, Keeper of the Book! I think the Magical Kingdom of Birds is in danger again.'

Chapter Two

'Hold on tight, Maya,' said Patch, as they flew through the noisy, hot, green-lit forest towards a stage. It had obviously been raining recently—waxy-leaved branches dripped water on them as Patch flew under the trees, but after the first surprise Maya quite liked it. She thought it was very beautiful to see patches of sunlight shine down through the forest canopy and light up fronds of palms growing on the forest floor.

More and more songbirds joined them as they flew, whistling and calling with joy as they went.

Maybe Willow is right. Maybe her uncle really has turned over a new leaf, thought Maya. *It would be so nice for her.*

They suddenly emerged into a clearing. A waterfall fell from a height from cliffs behind a stage, and as the water fell into a pool the sunlight caught it and made rainbows. It was a beautiful scene, but noisy, as even the sound of the water was drowned out by the whistles and trills of all the assembled songbirds. The sun was very bright and Maya blinked.

'Here Maya, wear these when the sun is too bright,' said Willow, flying towards her alongside another fairy. She still had her little sparkling coronet on but now she was also wearing a pair of sunglasses with the frame made out of thin willow and the lens made out of translucent leaves. She was holding out another pair of sunglasses for Maya.

'Welcome Maya!' said the two fairies who were with her. Their skin was freckled brown, like a song thrush's feathers, and their hair was as red as a robin's breast.

'My name is Aria,' said the girl fairy, 'and my twin brother is called Arioso.' The boy fairy nodded and smiled at Maya.

'The sunlight here is very strong, so I have a special cream for you both to put on your skin so it doesn't burn. I made it from coconut and tropical fern. I use it myself when we come to visit the songbirds who live here,' Arioso said.

'Thank you!' said Willow, and took some cream from the little pot made of plaited leaves and passed it to Maya, who put some on too.

'Oh! I can see a laughingthrush!' said Willow, delighted. 'I adore listening to them sing. I must go and chat to them before they go on stage.'

She flew off excitedly.

'Princess Willow is so glad about her uncle organizing this,' said Maya, raising her voice above the din. 'But Patch and I aren't sure we can trust him. What do you think, Aria and Arioso?'

'I'm not sure, either,' said Aria. 'I know he sent each bird an invitation and said that his dear niece Princess Willow would be here, and how much they would both appreciate the songbirds coming to sing in a new era in the Magical Kingdom. And there is nothing that songbirds love more than singing, so of course everybody has come, either to perform or to listen.'

'Everyone is so excited, it really does feel as though it's bringing us together. You will hear some wonderful performances today, I'm sure of it,' said Arioso, proudly. 'Come, take your seats. Lord Astor is about to introduce the acts.'

Maya slipped off Patch's back and sat on one of the huge flowers in front of the stage. Willow came and sat on the flower next to her and they both took off their sunglasses.

Lord Astor took to the stage. He looked very fancy in a sparkling cloak and bright shirt and trousers.

'Thank you so much for coming from all over the kingdom for this extravaganza of song, a celebration of the musical gifts you, the songbirds, enjoy. Thank you for nominating your best singers to stand up and entertain us today.

'It is so special for me to see my niece, Princess Willow, here. I wanted to organize this concert in her honour because I feel so deeply, deeply sorry for the misunderstandings there have been between us.'

'Hmm, are you, indeed?' said Patch quietly. 'Actions speak louder than words.'

'I was playing my flute,' continued Lord Astor, 'and remembering my sister, Princess Willow's dear mother, and the music touched my heart, and inspired me to organize this concert.' He whipped out a handkerchief and wiped his eyes.

'You see, he really is sorry,' whispered Willow to Maya and Patch.

'I would like, if I may, to be allowed the honour of accompanying each and every songbird representative on my flute, dedicating my performance to my niece, Princess Willow.'

'I knew he loved me really,' said

Willow, happily.

There were approving tweets, and chirps, and fluttering of feathers from the crowd.

'You really are my favourite birds in the whole kingdom!' he said, and the

songbirds responded with whoops and whistles. 'You're the best, you really are!' he continued. 'My guards and I hope you will never forget this concert, and please, enjoy the free berries and seeds my guards are distributing.'

'Songbirds are the best, it's true,' said Aria to Arioso, as they clapped Lord Astor.

'I don't like this,' said Maya to Patch and Willow.

'Neither do I,' said Patch. 'Everyone knows that we corvids are best.'

'No, that's not what I mean,' said Maya. 'Willow—you always say that all the birds are different but equally important to you. Don't you think that there is something strange with how Lord Astor is flattering the songbirds? There's something wrong here. I think he is up to something.'

'No, didn't you see him crying? He is really sorry. I'm sure Uncle is just trying to be encouraging and nice,' said Willow. 'Maybe he just means that songbirds are the best singers—and that's true, of course.' But she sounded as though she was trying to convince herself.

'My niece is frowning. Don't you agree that songbirds are the best birds, Princess Willow?' said Lord Astor. 'Come, join me on the stage.'

Princess Willow flew up on to the stage next to her uncle.

'I'm delighted to be here,' she said, smiling. 'I absolutely love singing myself and I can't wait to hear you, the real experts.'

The songbirds all chirped, and warbled, and called in delight as Princess Willow beamed and waved at them. She looked so regal—a real princess. Maya thought that Lord Astor didn't look too pleased at Willow's tactful speech, but he covered it up well.

'Diplomatic as always,' he said. 'So, without further ado, let's get on with the show,' announced Lord Astor, clapping as he escorted Willow to a seat on the stage next to him, and a beautiful white bird with a blue eye mask and fantastic white hair tufts took the stage. Its long, white tail had black markings.

'It's a Bali mynah bird!' said Maya. 'They are really rare in my world, I've read all about them.'

'It's a starling,' said Patch, a bit dismissively.

'Yes, I remember that—it's also called a Bali starling,' said Maya. 'It's really special.'

Patch looked a bit upset.

'Not more special than you, of course,' said Maya, quickly. Patch could be very sensitive. 'You're the only one of you there is, Patch. My best magpie friend.'

The white mynah bird did a sort of chattering song, full of whistles and sounds, a bit like a musical conversation. It bobbed its head as it sang, and Maya really liked it. So did the crowd—they clapped and whistled, but the other mynahs in the audience made the most noise. He was their favourite.

Lord Astor took a silver flute out of a case, leaving it open on the stage, so Maya could see all the sheets of white paper inside it. *It's the same as the picture in the book*! thought Maya. Willow looked so pleased to see her uncle holding the flute, she got up and gave him a hug in front of everyone.

'Look at his face,' said Patch, leaning in to speak to Maya. He looked genuinely surprised and pleased to be hugged. But then Maya saw him glance at Willow's crown and look angry and jealous for a moment, to be quickly replaced by his normal sneering smile.

'Everybody!' said Willow, standing on the stage beside her uncle. 'I am so happy to see that my uncle has brought his flute along. I loved hearing him accompany my mother when she sang.'

Willow looked so radiant and pleased as she flew back to sit on her flower, but Maya did not feel as confident.

'He's up to something, I'm sure of it,' said Patch.

The mynah birds wanted to hear more, and were screeching 'Encore! Encore!' and so the Bali mynah began to sing again. It was quite hard to hear, as this time Lord Astor was accompanying him on flute and all you could hear were the enthusiastic calls of the audience and the liquid sounds of the flute.

'Lord Astor is really good, isn't he?' said Aria, clapping and smiling. 'I'm so happy he has organized this concert. There will be harmony again in our kingdom, I am sure.'

Astor stopped playing.

'Thank you, fellow musicians. Thank you Mr Mynah. Please take your place backstage until we all meet up for the final number.'

'The mynah bird doesn't look very happy, does he?' said Patch in Maya's ear, as the mynah was led offstage by Lord Astor's guards.

'Something doesn't feel right, we must keep our eyes and ears open.'

Chapter Three

'And now a duet by two magnificent green magpies!' announced Lord Astor.

They were very dramatic, putting lots of energy into the vast range of calls they made. They reminded Maya of Saffron's brother Theo and his class rehearsing for the school concert. They had to play chimes and rattles and washboards and slide whistles. The whistles made such a funny sound they made everyone laugh, but their kind teacher Miss Haynes couldn't tell them off too much.

Like Theo and his class, the green magpies were having so much fun it was impossible not to smile.

Maybe Theo's class should all wear green suits and black masks for the concert, thought Maya.

When the audience flapped their wings and called out for more, Astor put his flute to his lips and played along with the magpies.

'It's strange, it's like with the mynah bird—as soon as Astor plays I can't hear the birds' song,' said Maya to Patch. 'And look at the way Lord Astor's guards are practically pushing them offstage.'

There was no doubt that Lord Astor was very good at playing the flute, and as he blew into it the music which came out of it, like his words, affected everyone. As each performer came and went the

audience grew a little quieter.

It doesn't feel happy quiet though, thought Maya.

One of the birds next to her passed a leaf with some berries and seeds to Maya. Maya was about to take one when she looked at the little bird's eyes. They were very heavy.

Patch turned to take a berry and Maya knocked the leaf so that the berries dropped.

'Don't eat the snacks, Patch. I think there's something wrong. Look at how sleepy some of the birds in the audience seem.'

Two little yellow canaries came on and peeped a very loud, high, pretty song, and a nightingale sang lots of rich high and low notes one after the other, but both songs were drowned out as soon as Lord Astor played the flute with them, and the birds were led off the stage by the guards.

Next came the white-crested laughingthrush.

'Oh, I absolutely love this bird's song,' said Arioso, clapping his hands. 'It makes me so happy! And they are such friendly, trusting little birds.'

The laughingthrush began singing, a sweet high whistle. First it sang in single notes and then it threw back its head and white throat and pointed its little black beak up as it did a faster whistling song in a repeated pattern. It sounded and looked like it was throwing back its head to laugh and it made Maya forget her worries and want to giggle. It sang as if it was having the best time ever and everybody chortled and guffawed alongside. Lord Astor played the flute with it for the encore—and he even made his flute sound like it was laughing along with the laughingthrush.

'But why is it that Lord Astor's playing doesn't make me happy like the birdsong does? He is better than Saffron at playing the flute, but I like listening to her more too. Maybe his music is like his words— they both sound good, but the feeling they both leave behind is miserable,' whispered Maya to Patch.

Then she noticed something. Instead

of throwing his head back to laugh, showing his lovely white throat, the little thrush put his black beak down and was staring at Lord Astor as if he was confused.

As the laughingthrush was led offstage by the guards, Arioso grabbed Maya's hand. 'Something is wrong,' he said. 'The laughingthrush wasn't laughing at the end.'

'I agree with Arioso,' said Aria. 'Something is wrong. I know that particular little laughingthrush—his name is Lufti and he is so kind, and gentle, and jolly, and once he starts laughing he finds it hard to stop—it's impossible that he would stop laughing so quickly. But even with the sound of the flute you could see from the way he was standing that he wasn't singing his laughing song at the end at all.'

'Well, why don't we go backstage to check up on him?' said Maya. 'Lord Astor said there would be an interval now—look—he is giving out more of those seeds and berries to the audience.'

'Good idea,' said Princess Willow as she joined them. 'I am a bit worried about Lufti, and I would like to thank the performers for their wonderful songs. They are all so good and so different.'

Maya and Willow, Patch, Aria, and Arioso made their way backstage.

First they saw all the birds still waiting to go on. They were busy and noisy, doing lots of warm-up exercises for their voices and checking each other's feathers. There was a very excited atmosphere, although there was a little row going on between the robins and a grey and brown lyrebird with a delicate plumed tail.

'It's not fair, Nathan, if you sing part of our song,' said one robin. 'You keep stealing everyone's tunes.'

'Calm down. I'm a lyrebird—that's what I do,' said the lyrebird. 'I hear sounds and I copy them and mix them into a musical arrangement. It's nothing personal. I am going to sing snatches of everyone's songs—it will only be a sample of yours. Listen—this is what I've heard so far.'

He puffed out his chest and began to sing. There was a snatch of a warbling birdsong and Lord Astor's laugh.

'You're a recording bird!' said Maya.

'Hmm, I don't like the sound of Lord Astor's laugh,' said Patch grimly. 'It's as nasty as it always was.'

'That's not fair. He's changed, I tell you,' said Princess Willow, crossly. 'It wasn't nasty. He was just laughing because he is happy we are all friends again.'

'Actually, Princess Willow, I'm a bit worried,' said the lyrebird. 'My friend Lufti went on, and he said he'd come back and tell me how it went, and he hasn't. Do you know where the performers go once they have performed?'

'I have no idea,' said Willow. 'Does anyone know?'

All the other birds shook their heads.

'I'm not on until last,' said the lyrebird. 'I'll go and look for him.'

The start of the second half of the

show was announced, and everyone took their places again, Willow next to her uncle on the stage, and Maya and Patch on flowers near the edge of the stage.

The first act after the interval was the white-rumped shama singing an absolutely beautiful song—whistling and chirping, its clear, melodious notes rising and falling, its long black and white tail longer than its little black and chestnut body.

Then Lord Astor took up his flute to play for the encore. At first Maya could hear him keeping up with all the fast and varied liquid notes the shama sang. She could hear both the shama's song and Lord Astor's flute in harmony. Then, as a shaft of bright sunlight broke through the leafy canopy, Patch whispered urgently in Maya's ear.

'Look Maya—look at the shama's beak and then the end of Astor's flute. Something is sparkling.'

Maya looked, and saw, from out of the open beak of the shama bird, a series of tiny sparkling musical notes, just like the notes drawn around the edges of the pages in the book. They were streaming from the beak of the bird into the sparkling silvery flute. Willow's Uncle Astor was dancing around and the bright sunlight was reflecting from the shiny flute's surface so that you had to have the sharp eye of a magpie to notice the tiny sparkling line.

And suddenly, you could only hear Lord Astor's flute again.

Then the bewildered-looking shama was ushered quickly off the stage by Lord Astor's guards.

Maya and Patch looked at each other.

'He's . . .' stuttered Maya, struggling to believe what she was seeing. 'He's taking their voices. We have to do something!'

Just then Nathan came back.

'Come with me,' he said, and they slipped away behind the stage, to a hidden area behind the waterfall.

He opened his beak and they heard the

shama's voice saying: 'No, I follow Princess Willow, not you', and then the sound of falling water, then a swishing curtain.

'I couldn't find my friend Lufti, but I followed the guards and saw them taking the shama here to the waterfall,' said Nathan. 'A guard saw me so I couldn't follow. He has gone now, here's our chance to have a look.'

Maya and Patch looked around, and Maya discovered some vines hanging down.

'These could have made the swishing noise!' she said and, looking around to make sure no guards were following, pulled the curtain of vines aside. It made the same swishing noise Nathan had picked up. And there, hidden from the stage and the eyes of the crowd, in a little cavern, were rows of cages with unhappy, silent songbirds locked inside. They opened their beaks but they could not make any noise to tell what had happened.

'This is terrible!' gasped Maya. 'I knew Willow's Uncle Astor wasn't to be trusted! I think he has been trying to flatter the songbirds into following him, not Princess Willow, and he has magically stolen their voices when they don't agree.'

'Thank you, songbirds, for your loyalty to Princess Willow,' said Patch. 'We will get your voices back, I promise!'

'We have got to warn Willow and stop the concert!' said Maya. 'Let's go back to the stage and see if we can attract her attention.'

They flew back to the stage and looked with horror at the scene.

Princess Willow was up on the stage, singing, and Lord Astor was accompanying her on the flute!

Chapter Four

Willow was performing the beautiful lullaby that she had sung to Maya earlier. But as she came to the line beginning 'Brave adventures' she touched her throat in bewilderment—she couldn't sing the words, 'friendship too', and, as he played, Lord Astor sneered as he saw her face.

'Don't worry, Willow, I am your friend

and I will save you,' promised Maya out loud, even though her friend couldn't hear her. She had a plan forming in her head, but she needed help.

Patch took Maya back to her seat, and she began to whisper to the songbird fairies. 'Arioso—go with Nathan and release the birds before the guards realize what you are doing, and Aria, go to those still waiting to go on and warn them to escape with you—bring them all into the audience and wait there for instructions,' said Maya. 'Hurry!'

The fairies rushed away as Willow was ushered off the stage. Lord Astor looked very pleased with himself.

'We have to get on the stage and tell the audience exactly what is happening!'

said Patch. 'Climb on my back and I will fly up there.'

Before Maya had time to think, she and Patch were on the stage next to Lord Astor, in front of everyone.

'Who let these two on the stage?' said Lord Astor, furiously. 'Guards—take them off!'

'Say something, Maya,' said Patch, but Maya looked at all the birds facing her, opened her mouth and got so stage-struck she couldn't say a word.

'Maya?' said Patch, but Maya just couldn't say anything—it was as if Astor had taken her voice too.

'Oh, I'll do it,' he said, and he began to call out loudly. 'Listen, everyone—Lord Astor has imprisoned all the songbirds who sang for you and stolen

77

their voices, and now he has stolen Princess Willow's voice too.'

There were distressed gasps, and calls, and flutterings from the crowd, but it was very muted. The birds in the audience seemed very weak.

Suddenly some guards ran on, waving their arms about, followed by an angry Aria and Arioso.

'Patch is right—he imprisoned the songbirds, but we have just released them!' There was a crowd of angry songbirds behind them, hovering in the air, glaring at Lord Astor, but all silent.

Lufti the laughingthrush was there, and Nathan too, looking worried for his silent friend.

Lord Astor flew up into the air with his flute as Maya climbed on Patch's back.

'I wouldn't do anything silly if I were you. I'm the only one who can give you your songs back.'

The guards approached Patch and Maya but Lord Astor waved them away.

'No, leave them. It will give me great pleasure to explain to everyone my plan; it is too clever to keep to myself. Yes, I imprisoned the songbirds and took their songs because they kept on insisting that Princess Willow is the true ruler of the Magical Kingdom of Birds. And I have taken my niece's voice because, frankly, I am sick of hearing it, and the great thing is that I have fixed it so they will never get their songs back until they all—including dear little Willow—accept I am their leader. And once they do accept me as their leader, all the other birds in the kingdom will follow, I am sure.'

'What do you mean, they will never get their songs back?' said Maya, furiously, as she and Patch rose in the air, level with

Willow's triumphant, wicked uncle.

'I have enchanted the flute. It took each note and now, look. Guards—bring me the paper.

Lord Astor took the flute and shook it over the paper the guards held, so that the silver notes streamed out onto the sheets.

'Here are all your songs, songbirds. But my enchanted flute has changed them into written notes, and as you can't read music, you will only hear your songs again when I play them on my flute. Your voices will only be released when your tunes are played. And I will only do that when you admit that I, and only I, am the rightful ruler of the Magical Kingdom!'

'What about the birds in the audience and the ones who haven't yet gone on?' said Patch. 'Can't they just sing their tunes back to them? They know their songs already. You didn't think of that, did you?'

Lord Astor threw back his head and laughed, a nasty cackling laugh, nothing like the laughingthrush's joyful sound.

'Of course I did! Why do you think I gave them all enchanted berries? They are so weak now they don't even remember their own names, never mind how to sing, and only the sound of their own birdsong will cure them. And they will only hear THAT when I play it back to them, and only I can read the music.'

'You have a niece who wants to love you. You are so talented and have so much already,' said Maya, angrily. 'Why are you doing this?'

Lord Astor looked sulky. 'Because I am the best. I am better than the rest.' He looked at his flute and smirked. 'I really and truly am the cleverest of the clever. I have an ENORMOUS brain. They need me to be their leader. And now they HAVE to accept me or there will be a silent spring, summer, autumn, and winter throughout the kingdom.' He glared at Maya and Patch.

'So get out of that, why don't you? Unless you can personally sing all the birds' songs, I don't think you have anything to contribute, do you?'

'We can't—but I know someone who can,' said Maya. 'Nathan—you are a performer so they mustn't have given you any berries—it's time for you to perform!'

'With pleasure!' said the lyrebird, and opened his beak.

'Stop him!' said the guards as they realized what Nathan was about to do, but immediately a crowd of fluttering silent birds flew in front of Nathan, protecting him from the guards.

From the side of the stage flew two enraged green magpies who headed directly to Lord Astor and knocked the flute from his hands before he had a chance to blow it. Patch swooped quickly down and Maya caught it with the curved edges of her sticks.

The Javan green magpies circled Lord Astor whilst Nathan the lyrebird began to sing, and Patch and Maya snatched the music manuscript paper with the shining silver notes on it from the surprised guards. The other birds flew around Patch and Maya to protect them. They couldn't tell Lord Astor in their usual noisy way what they thought of him, but their body language was clear.

'Thank you for your quick thinking!' called Maya to the green magpies, the flute and the music safe in her arms, and they gave her cheeky winks.

Nathan the lyrebird, in the meantime, was singing the songs of all the birds, and as he sang the air filled with sparkling musical notes, streaming from the sheets of paper in Maya's hands back to each bird in turn.

The silver notes still stayed on the paper, but as the lyrebird sang, each note released more of the birds in the crowd. It was so pretty to watch the notes fly back into the birds' mouths until they could sing again, healing them and making them strong.

Lord Astor hovered in the air, still

smirking.

'Haven't you forgotten someone?' he said to Maya, snatching the sheets of music out of her hands. He shuffled through the pages until he found the last one, and triumphantly held it up. 'Look—there's a rather important sheet of paper with a rather special song written down.'

He held it up. It said 'Princess Willow's Lullaby'.

The crowd of birds on the stage parted as two guards marched Willow back onto the stage.

'So, birds,' taunted Lord Astor. 'You

say you love your darling Princess Willow SO much, but I can tell you, she will never get her voice back unless you say you love me more than her.'

All the birds tweeted and chirped unhappily. Maya could see Willow trembling, and just wanted to put her arms around her.

'I think I can solve this,' whispered Maya to Aria. 'Please—tell him you love him more than Princess Willow, and get all the birds to say the same.'

'Never!' said Aria. 'I don't love him and I don't trust him. Even if we say we love him he won't give the Princess her voice back, I am sure.'

'Please, trust me. I think I know what I must do,' whispered Maya. 'He has to let down his guard— I have to get that sheet of music back from him and get Princess Willow her song back.'

Chapter Five

'Lord Astor,' called Aria. 'We, the songbird fairies, call on all the songbirds in the kingdom to accept you as the leader!'

There was a surprised outcry from the birds, but Arioso waved his arms to quieten them down, and Aria continued speaking, flying in the air facing Lord

Astor. All the birds could see her fingers were crossed behind her back as she said, 'Lord Astor, I think you are our rightful ruler.'

'Lord Astor, I think you are our rightful ruler,' said Arioso, his fingers crossed too.

'Lord Astor, I think you are our rightful ruler,' said Nathan the clever lyrebird quickly, his tail slightly crossed.

'Lord Astor, you are just the best,' lied the magpies, crossing their eyes, but Lord Astor was so excited that he didn't notice. Maya wanted to giggle but managed to hold it in. She could hear Willow give a sad sniff as she sat in front of her and she gave her a little hug.

'Princess Willow, don't worry—look at everyone as they say the words,' she whispered.

'Lord Astor, I think you are our rightful ruler,' repeated one bird after another in the line, but every bird managed to cross something—either their tail feathers or wings or their feet or even their eyes, like the cheeky magpies, and Lord Astor was so puffed up by his success that he didn't suspect anything.

'Let me take those messy papers from

you and sort them out,' said Aria, sweetly, and took them off Lord Astor and quietly passed them to Maya.

'Thank you, fairy,' said Lord Astor and flew up in the air to hover in front of Patch.

'What about you, magpie?' he said. 'You are always hanging around with my niece. What do you say? You are the last bird here and I want to hear from you before I give her back her voice. Then she can get lost. She isn't wanted here, and should go away with this strange little wingless fairy she hangs around with.'

'Of course you are the best,' fibbed Patch, crossing his feet in the air.

'So—all of you have come to your senses!' exclaimed Lord Astor, rubbing his hands in delight. 'It's a shame it took so long, but I knew you would come round in the end. Songbirds really ARE my favourites. I won't forget this.'

'So can Princess Willow have her voice back now?' said Aria.

'Oh, of course!' said Lord Astor.

There was an excited chirping, but then he raised his hand and put on a mock sad face.

'Oh dear, I forgot, how terribly sad. You see, my niece, not being a songbird, chose to sing the words and music of the lullaby her mother sang her. She had some silly sentimental attachment to it. What a shame. The music will never be released because, I am afraid, there is nothing I can do. I'm only a flautist, not a singer. Nobody but Princess Willow knows the lullaby, so nobody but Princess Willow can sing it, and I am afraid that our lyrebird friend and my flute can mimic birdsong, but cannot sing words like a fairy can.'

'I've heard it and I think, with the help of the sheet music, I can remember how to sing it,' said Maya, startling Lord Astor. Aria the fairy was hiding his flute so he couldn't get it back, and was protected by a great crowd of birds again.

'I think I can remember most of the tune, and Saffron told me that the written notes are there to remind me of it—I can see when they go up and go down, and how long they are,' said Maya, so she looked at the silver notes and, gathering up all her courage, she began to sing, in front of all the birds and the fairies:

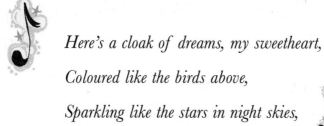

Here's a cloak of dreams, my sweetheart,
Coloured like the birds above,
Sparkling like the stars in night skies,
Feather-soft and full of love.

Silver notes began to leave the last
page, and as Maya's confidence grew
the sparkling notes flew back into
Willow's mouth. Willow turned, with
her hands at her throat and a huge smile
on her face, and she sang the last verse
with Maya:

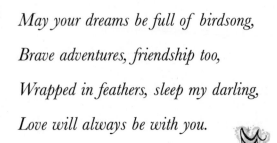

May your dreams be full of birdsong,
Brave adventures, friendship too,
Wrapped in feathers, sleep my darling,
Love will always be with you.

They gave each other a delighted hug and Willow, her strength and courage back with her voice, flew up into the air. All the birds exploded into delighted chirps, and whoops, and cries, and whistles, and the forest glade was full of ecstatic birdsong. Maya sat on a branch next to the Javan green magpies as their song filled the air, joining the incredible choir of all of the birds singing together.

'We love you Princess Willow,' they all sang. 'You are the best!'

Lord Astor screamed in temper, snatched the flute from Aria and broke it in two. He grabbed the sheets of paper with silver notes on and ripped them up, waving his fist. 'But you still don't have the magic cloak of feathers, so don't celebrate too soon! Come guards!' and he flew off.

The magpies went to chase them, but Willow signalled for them to stop.

'Thank you all, you beautiful singers and Aria and Arioso. Thank you Nathan the lyrebird and Patch and Maya, the Keeper of the Book. It is so lovely to have my voice back. But my uncle is right, until I have all the feathers for my cloak I cannot get back the throne,' Willow said, sadly. 'I'm sorry I didn't listen to you from the start, Maya. I just wanted so desperately for my uncle to be telling the truth. You saved us all with your bravery, and with your song.'

Maya had never felt so proud.

'Let us give you a green feather for the cloak on behalf of all the songbirds of the kingdom,' said the Javan green magpies.

'Thank you, songbirds,' said Princess Willow, and then turned to Maya and handed it to her. 'Please Maya, this is the end of this particular brave adventure, but I know there will be more to share. And whatever comes, you will always have my thanks and my friendship.'

'Mine too,' said Patch, over his shoulder.

'And ours,' sang all the birds.

'And ours!' said Aria and Arioso, coming over to hug Maya.

Maya carefully opened the book and put the green feather inside, where it changed into a drawing. She slipped off Patch's back, and, leaning on her willow sticks, she gave Patch and Willow a hug.

'I'll miss you two,' she said, sadly.

'Love will always be with you,' whispered Willow, and put something in Maya's bag. Then all Maya could see were sparkling green feathers and all she could hear was birdsong, until she found herself lying on her bed in her bedroom, her book beside her, her satchel hanging over the back of her chair.

'Time for dinner!' called Penny.

***

'How are you feeling, Maya?' said Saffron. It was the concert. Theo's class had performed and everyone had clapped, and Saffron had sung her solo beautifully, and then come straight over to check that Maya was feeling all right.

'I'm scared, but I know that's normal,'

said Maya, smiling at her kind friend. 'You were great. I'm just going to do my best.'

Maya knew if she could sing in front of songbirds she could sing anywhere—and if she could sing in front of wicked Lord Astor, she could certainly sing in front of friends and family who loved her.

'Good luck, Maya! You'll be great! I love your friend's song about the feathered cloak!' said Saffron. 'I'd love to learn to sing it too. The music on the page she gave you looks so lovely too—it's so sparkly!'

'I'll teach it to you,' promised Maya, smiling.

Then she went out onto the stage, opened her mouth, and started to sing.

Acknowledgements

I am so lucky to be working with the amazing
illustrator Rosie Butcher on this series, and for
it to be designed so gorgeously by Lizzie Smart.
I am so proud that this book is so beautiful,
and that's because of them.

Thank you to Liz Cross, Clare Whitston, and
Debbie Sims for your amazing support,
encouragement, and editing of The Magical
Kingdom of Birds books.

Thank you to Hannah Penny from OUP, who
came with me and my husband and daughter to
Waddesdon Manor when I gave a talk about the
Magical Kingdom of Birds series, saw the
wonderful birds there, and learnt about the
conservation work the team at Waddesdon Manor
does. Thank you for looking after us, Hannah.

Thank you to everyone at Waddesdon Manor
for your welcome and hospitality—we had such
a lovely day.

Thank you to the lovely parents and children
I met at Waddesdon that day, I enjoyed meeting
you all so much. I hope you enjoy this.

Thank you to Fraser Hutchinson at OUP and
everyone who works with this series.

Thank you, as always, to my friend Helen Sole,
play therapist, teacher, athlete who played in the
Great Britain sitting volleyball team, for advice in
this series on Maya's problems with her legs.

I would like to thank the lovely Anne Clark, my
agent. I get to write so many lovely books like this
because of her! I am very lucky.

Lastly, thank you to my family, and especially to
Graeme, my lovely husband, and to the songbirds
who sing outside my window every day!

About Anne

Every Christmas, Anne used to ask for a dog. She had to wait many years, but now she has two dogs, called Timmy and Ben. Timmy is a big, gentle golden retriever who loves people and food and is scared of cats. Ben is a small brown and white cavalier King Charles spaniel who is a bit like a cat because he curls up in the warmest places and bosses Timmy about. He snuffles and snorts quite a lot, and you can tell what he is feeling by the way he walks. He has a particularly pleased patter when he has stolen something he shouldn't have, which gives him away immediately. Anne lives in a village in Kent and is not afraid of spiders.

About Rosie

Rosie lives in a little town in East Yorkshire with her husband and daughter. She draws and paints by night, but by day she builds dens on the sofa, watches films about princesses, and attends tea parties. Rosie enjoys walking and having long conversations with her little girl, Penelope. They usually discuss important things like spider webs, birds, and prickly leaves.

Bird Fact File

Turn the page for information
on the real-life birds that
inspired this story.

Fun Facts

1. There are around 5,000 different species of songbird.

2. Songbirds make up nearly half the world's bird species.

3. Songbirds' vocal organs develop differently to other birds, which means they are able to produce a more varied and complex song.

4. A bird's vocal organ is called a syrinx.

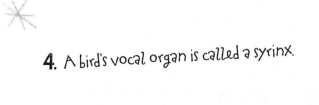

5. Bird songs are different to bird calls.
All birds call to warn of danger (known as
'alarm calls') or to say hello (known as
'contact calls'), but only songbirds sing.

6. Bird songs are generally long and complex,
whilst bird calls are short and simple.

7. Songbirds sing mainly to impress other birds, and to defend their territory by showing how strong and healthy they are.

8. In many bird species only the male birds sing.

9. In the tropics however many female birds do sing, and some species sing duets together!

10. Most birds sing while perched up high in their territory, but some, such as buntings and skylarks, sing while they're flying.

11. Some songbirds have the ability to sing two notes at once, and can even sing rising and falling notes at the same time!

12. Most birds have to learn to sing by listening to the adults around them, they are not born knowing how.

13. Songbirds can have regional accents, just like people!

14. Lyrebirds are capable of imitating almost any sound – they have been recorded mimicking chainsaws, camera shutters, dogs barking, phones ringing, and even the human voice.

Where do you find
songbirds?

Find out more about some of the real-life songbirds in the story, with thanks to our friends at Waddesdon Manor aviary!

Bali Starling
(Leucopsar rothschildi)

CRITICALLY ENDANGERED

Personality: Confident, family orientated.

Threats: Poaching for illegal songbird trade. This is made worse by habitat loss.

Distribution: Northwest Bali, with a small population introduced on the small island of Nusa Penida.

Habitat: Forest edges including open shrub savannahs and flooded savannah woodlands.

Diet: Seeds, insects, fruits, and occasionally small reptiles.

Lifespan: Five years in the wild, but can live for up to fifteen years in captivity.

Number of young: Clutches often have two to three eggs, but normally only one survives.

Interesting fact: The Bali starling is the national bird of Bali. Nearly extinct in the wild, breeding and reintroduction programmes saved them.

Javan Green Magpie
(Cissa thalassina)

CRITICALLY ENDANGERED

Personality: Intelligent and curious.

Threats: Habitat loss and degradation, driven by agricultural expansion, logging, and mining. Poaching for illegal songbird trade.

Distribution: Western Java, Indonesia.

Habitat: Mountain forests, occasionally ranging into lowland areas.

Diet: Mostly invertebrates and small vertebrates, including frogs and lizards.

Lifespan: Unknown.

Number of young: Usually one or two individuals.

Interesting fact: The bright green plumage is attained through the birds' diet. If not kept correctly they can turn blue.

White-rumped Shama
(Kittacincla malabarica)

Personality: Arrogant.

Threats: Poaching for illegal songbird trade. This is made worse by habitat loss.

Distribution: Large range extending from northern India, Nepal, and southern China and Indonesia.

Habitat: Lowland tropical moist forest, swamp forest.

Diet: Insects, worms, and berries.

Lifespan: Nine to twelve years.

Number of young: Three or five individuals.

Interesting fact: Thought to be the best singing songbird on earth.

Sumatran Laughingthrush
(Garrulax bicolor)

ENDANGERED

Personality: Shy, but vocal if startled. A little mischievous too.

Threats: Poaching for illegal songbird trade. This is made worse by habitat loss.

Distribution: Originally distributed along the length of Sumatra, Indonesia. However, recent evidence suggests they have become fragmented after undergoing considerable decline.

Habitat: Middle and lower stories of mountainous forest.

Diet: Mainly insects, including beetles and spiders.

Lifespan: Unknown.

Number of young: Two to three individuals.

Interesting fact: Considered to be cooperative breeders, meaning chicks receive care from additional group members, as well as their parents.

Asian Songbird Crisis

In Southeast Asia, birds are favourite family pets because of their songs and beautiful colours. Many of these birds were born in the forest and caught in traps by poachers, then sold in markets. There are not many left in the forest now. Zoos and other charities, such as the European Association of Zoos and Aquaria (EAZA) Silent Forest campaign, are trying to stop these birds going extinct in the wild. Find out more at www.silentforest.eu

A note from the author:

I love birds and watching them in real life and reading about them in books and online. Every day I enjoy listening to birds singing, either as I lie in bed in the morning, or when I take my dogs Timmy and Ben for walks in the countryside near us.

When writing this book I included some particular songbirds I saw in the Waddesdon Manor Aviary, as you'll have seen from the factfile, and I also read about them and watched videos about them online. You can find out lots on Waddesdon Manor's web page: *https://waddesdon.org.uk/your-visit/grounds/aviary/*

I have also discovered another wonderful songbirds' conservation project at Chester Zoo, which I hope to visit one day, and

I downloaded the song they have released to help conserve songbirds. You can read about this here: *https://www.actforwildlife.org.uk/what-we-fight-for/conservation-challenges/our-campaigns/sing-for-songbirds/*

Join Maya for another adventure in

The Missing Fairy-Wrens

Spring is in the air, the flowers are
blooming, and Maya is excited to meet the
tiny fairy-wrens in the Magical Kingdom
of Birds. But something's wrong: half
the birds have gone missing. Can this be
another of Lord Astor's despicable plans?
And can Maya and her friends stop him
before it's too late?

Magical kingdom
of Birds
The Missing Fairy-Wrens

ANNE BOOTH

Illustrated by Rosie Butcher

Chapter One

'You're so good at swimming!' said Maya's friend, Saffron, to her.

'How do you swim so fast?' said Theo, Saffron's brother.

Maya, Theo, and Saffron were drinking hot chocolate together at Saffron and Theo's house after going swimming together. They were new neighbours and went to Maya's school, and all three had quickly become the best of friends.

'I've just done a lot of swimming, that's all,' said Maya. 'It helps my legs get stronger—it's so much easier for me to swim than walk really—my legs don't get as tired in the water.'

'And you are so good at horse riding too!' said Theo. 'I wish I could ride like you.'

'I'll take you next time,' said Maya, smiling at them. 'Penny and Dad said I should invite you to come with us to thank you for today. I'm so glad you've moved opposite me.'

'We're glad too!' said Saffron, beaming.

'So are you warmed up now after swimming?' said Emma, Saffron and Theo's mum. 'Is it a good time for me to teach you how to make paper flowers?'

Theo took the dirty cups out to the kitchen and brought three clean cups back. Then his mum, Emma, put out lots of lovely coloured paper onto the table. She showed them how to make a circle by drawing around a cup, and then she cut it out. Next she demonstrated how to cut a spiral in a circle, and then roll it

around a pencil, so they each had made
a beautiful rose.

'Thanks, Mum!' said Saffron. Emma
left them to it, as the three friends made
more and more flowers.

'I'm going to give some to our aunty for her birthday,' said Theo.

'I'm going to do that too,' said Saffron.

'Do you think I could make a bunch of them for Penny and Dad?' said Maya, as she finished making a rose. 'It's their wedding anniversary tomorrow. My big sister Lauren is coming back from university as a surprise and we are making a special meal for them, but I'd like to decorate the room too. I want them to feel special.'

'That's a great idea!' Theo said. 'I'll go and ask Mum for some more sheets of coloured paper for you to take home.'

'You can put them in the lovely satchel your mum gave you,' Saffron added, giving Maya a hug, as Theo came back with a big pile of coloured paper.

Maya had brought the satchel her mum had given her over to show Saffron and Theo. She couldn't remember her mum—Penny was her lovely stepmum—so it meant a lot to have had this satchel as a present from her. She was very proud of it and wanted to show her new friends. She hadn't told them about the magic colouring book and pencils her mum had put in the bag though—she had left them on her desk at home.

It was a little difficult to explain to Saffron and Theo that she wasn't just their school friend, Maya, she was also the Keeper of a magic book. When she was needed by her friends, Princess Willow, the fairy, and Patch, the talking magpie, a new picture would appear in the colouring book, and when she coloured it in she would be transported to the Magical Kingdom of Birds.

Maya said goodbye to her new friends and went back home. She hung the satchel over the back of her chair in her bedroom. Maya looked wistfully at the closed book on her desk. It had such a beautiful cover of deep-blue cloth, with lots of scenes of tiny gold birds flying, nesting, soaring, swooping in all sorts of places, all over it. In gold lettering on the front were the words *Magical Kingdom of Birds*.

'I wonder how Patch and Willow are,' Maya said out loud. 'I love my new friends, Saffron and Theo, but I miss Patch and Willow.' She had opened the book every day but there hadn't been a new page for a while, and without a page to colour in she couldn't get back to the kingdom to see her old friends.

She sat down and opened the satchel and took out the big wad of coloured paper Theo had given her to put inside. He and Saffron were so generous.

'I wonder if I could make some of the flowers I have seen in the Magical Kingdom of Birds?' she said. 'Even if there are no new pictures, at least I can look at the old ones I coloured in to give me some ideas. The flowers in the kingdom are so beautiful.'

As she reached to open the book to check the flowers she had coloured in before, she caught sight of a magpie hopping in the garden just outside her window. Every time she saw a magpie she thought of Patch, her friend. Maya felt a tingle of excitement when this one stopped and put his head on one side to look at her. He seemed to know her.

She opened the beautiful book to look at the pictures she had already done, but her heart started beating faster when she saw the book turn to a new page at last.

'They are calling me!' she said, and

looked for her pencils. 'Hooray! Hold on,
Princess Willow and Patch—I'm colouring
in the new page now! See you in the
Magical Kingdom of Birds!'

More magic awaits

Magical Kingdom
of Birds
The Missing Fairy-Wrens

ANNE BOOTH
Illustrated by Rosie Butcher

Magical Kingdom
of Birds
The Silent Songbirds

ANNE BOOTH
Illustrated by Rosie Butcher

Ready for more great stories?